A Mountain Hike

Acknowledgments

Executive Editor: Diane Sharpe

Supervising Editor: Stephanie Muller

Design Manager: Sharon Golden

Page Design: Simon Balley Design Associates

Photography: Heather Angel: cover (middle left), page 17;
Bruce Coleman: pages 11, 13, 15, 27; Greg Evans International
Photo Library: pages 24-25; The Image Bank: cover (middle right),
page 9; NHPA: cover (top right), pages 21, 22-23; Tony Stone
Associates: page 16.

ISBN: 0-8114-3793-0

A Mountain Hike

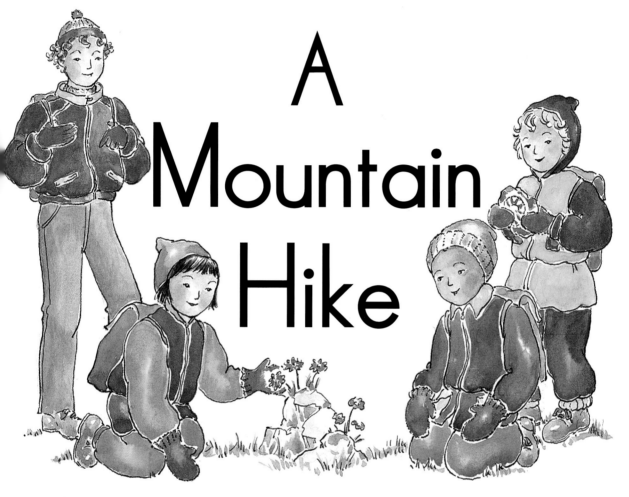

Paul Humphrey and
Alex Ramsay

Illustrated by
Kareen Taylerson

STECK-VAUGHN
COMPANY
ELEMENTARY · SECONDARY · ADULT · LIBRARY

My mom's taking us hiking
up the mountain.

4

We're all wearing hiking boots.

They have thick rubber soles so that we don't slip on the rocks.

What else do we need to take?

You need waterproof jackets and warm clothes. It will get colder as you go higher. You also need something to eat and drink.

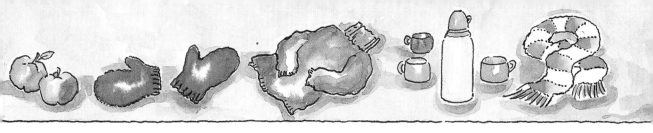

I've got some apples in my knapsack.

I've got a bottle of water.

7

You won't get lost if you stay on the path and use a map and compass.

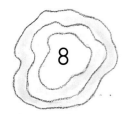

You can see where you are on a map. Use a compass to decide which direction to walk in.

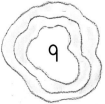

This used to be a quarry where rock was mined. It was used for building houses and roads.

Look! This rock has a shell in it!

10

That's not a real shell anymore. It's a
fossil. Millions of years ago, it was a
living creature. Now all that's left is the
shape of the shell in the stone.

I've found a beautiful, shiny rock.

This kind of rock is called quartz.

The water is cold because it is
melted snow.

Some mountains always have snow on the top. When the sun <u>shines</u>, the snow <u>melts</u>. Then the water forms streams that run down the mountain.

There are tiny plants
and flowers everywhere.

Those are alpine plants. They grow in
sheltered cracks in the rocks where they
won't be damaged by the strong winds
on the mountain.

It always gets colder as you climb higher up the mountain. That's why you brought extra clothes. Put your sweaters on now.

Why are the trees so small up here?

The trees are small because it's harder for them to grow here. There's only a very thin layer of soil covering the rocks.

18

Farther up the mountain, there won't be any trees at all. If you climb that high, you will be above the tree line.

That's a golden eagle. It's diving
on its prey.

It usually eats small animals, such as rabbits, but it has such strong talons that it can even kill foxes.

It has taken hundreds of years for the water to cut through the rock. The deep valley it has made is called a gorge.

This gorge is about 100 feet
deep. Did you know that parts of the
Grand Canyon are almost one mile deep?

The houses look tiny because they are so far below you. The higher you go, the smaller they look.

25

It's so cold on the mountaintop
that the ground is covered with
ice and snow all year.

26

During the winter, the whole mountain
is covered with snow.

27

It's time to go back down the mountain.
It's important to get to the bottom before
it gets dark.

I hope we can take
another mountain
hike sometime.

Can you name everything on this page? The answers are on the last page, but don't look until you have tried naming everything.

Index

Answers: 1. Mountaintop 2. Eagle 3. Stream 4. Quartz 5. Fossils

A Mountain Hike

THIS BOOK IS THE PROPERTY OF:

STATE _____	Book No. _____
PROVINCE _____	Enter information
COUNTY _____	in spaces
PARISH _____	to the left as
SCHOOL DISTRICT _____	instructed
OTHER _____	

ISSUED TO	Year Used	CONDITION	
		ISSUED	RETURNED
....	....	....	....
....	....	....	....

PUPILS to whom this textbook is issued must not write on any page or mark any part of it in any way, consumable textbooks excepted.

1. Teachers should see that the pupil's name is clearly written in ink in the spaces above in every book issued.
2. The following terms should be used in recording the condition of the book: New; Good; Fair; Poor; Bad.